BERTIE'S PICTURE DAY

Here are some other books
you will enjoy
by Pat Brisson and
Diana Cain Bluthenthal:

℮

Hot Fudge Hero
Little Sister, Big Sister

· PAT BRISSON ·

BERTIE'S PICTURE DAY

illustrated by

DIANA CAIN BLUTHENTHAL

Henry Holt and Company · New York

Henry Holt and Company, LLC, *Publishers since 1866*
115 West 18th Street, New York, New York 10011

Henry Holt is a registered trademark of Henry Holt and Company, LLC

Library of Congress Cataloging-in-Publication Data
Brisson, Pat.
Bertie's picture day / Pat Brisson; illustrated by Diana Cain Bluthenthal.
p.   cm.
Summary: Bertie tries to get spiffy for his class picture,
but several disastrous events result in his looking "interesting" instead.
[1. Beauty, Personal—Fiction. 2. Brothers and sisters—Fiction. 3. Schools—Fiction.]
I. Bluthenthal, Diana Cain, ill.   II. Title.
PZ7.B78046Ber   2000   [Fic]—dc21   00-22431

ISBN 0-8050-6281-5 / First Edition—2000
Printed in Mexico
1   3   5   7   9   10   8   6   4   2

Contents

Square Hole
3

Shiner
21

A Terribly Interesting Haircut
43

Picture Day
61

BERTIE'S PICTURE DAY

SQUARE HOLE

DUMB OLD TOOTH

Bertie had a loose tooth.

It was right in the front on the top.

He had already lost the tooth next to it.

He had lost the two bottom teeth, too.

Bertie wiggled the loose tooth

back and forth with his tongue.

He pushed it back and forth

with his bottom lip.

He poked it back and forth with his finger.

It hung on by a thread.

It would not fall out.

Every night Bertie checked in the mirror

to see if it was any closer to falling out.

"Come on, dumb old tooth,"
he whispered to it.
"Fall out!"

Every morning Bertie checked in the mirror
to see if maybe his tooth had fallen out
while he slept.
But no matter how hard he wiggled,
no matter how hard he pushed,
no matter how hard he poked,
that dumb old tooth hung on.
Every morning he said the same thing.
"Oh, fiddlesticks!
It's still there!"

ADVICE

At breakfast his father said,
"In the old days,
they said to tie one end of a string
around your loose tooth.
Then tie the other end
of the string around a doorknob.
Slam the door, and presto!
Out pops your tooth!"
"No, thanks," Bertie told him.
"I'll wait."

His mother said,
"Try not to think about it, Bertie.
A watched pot never boils."
But Bertie replied,

"This is not a pot.

It's a tooth.

And I don't want it to boil.

I want it to fall out.

Besides, it's very hard not to think about it."

Eloise, his little sister, said,

"My teeth are never going to fall out.

I won't let them."

"Everybody's teeth fall out, Eloise."

"Not mine," said Eloise.

"Yes, they will," said Bertie.

"No, they won't!" said Eloise.

"Will too!" said Bertie.

"Will NOT!" shouted Eloise.

"Bertie!" said his mother.

She gave him a look that meant,

Stop arguing this minute OR ELSE!

"Fine," said Bertie.

"Keep your old baby teeth."

"I am not a baby!" Eloise cried.

"Bertie," said his mother.

"It's time for you to go to school."

Bertie rolled his eyes,

picked up his backpack, and left.

MORE ADVICE

On the way to school, his friend Isobel said,
"Grab it with a tissue and give it a yank.
That's what I did when my tooth was loose."
"Well, maybe . . .," Bertie said.
But just thinking about that
made his tummy do flips
and made his hands get sweaty.
Bertie didn't think he was as brave as Isobel.

"Catch!" said Bertie's friend Howard.
He threw a kickball at Bertie's face.
It bounced hard off Bertie's nose.

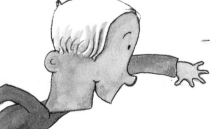

"Ouch!" cried Bertie, rubbing his nose.

"Oops!" said Howard.

"I was aiming for your mouth."

"You were aiming for my mouth?"
Bertie squealed. "Why?"

"I thought I could pop out
your loose tooth," Howard said.

"Oh!" said Bertie. "Good idea!"

He felt around his mouth with his tongue.

He shook his head.

"Nope. It's still there," he told Howard.

"Next time, aim lower."

STILL HANGING ON

All day long Bertie wiggled his tooth.
He wiggled it while he did math problems.
He wiggled it while he copied spelling words.
He wiggled it while he worked
on a science project.
But it kept hanging on.
It would not fall out.

At the end of the day,
his teacher, Mrs. Hughes,
passed out papers to everyone in the class.
"Monday is Picture Day," she said.
"Please take these papers home
to your parents.

They will need to fill out the forms
if they want to buy some pictures.
We will have our class picture taken, too.
So, remember to look spiffy!"

Just then the bell rang.
Bertie and his classmates took the papers.
They squished them into their backpacks.
Everyone hurried to get on line.
Molly raised her hand.
"Mrs. Hughes?" she called.
"What does *spiffy* mean?"
Mrs. Hughes smiled.
"Good question, Molly.
Does anyone know what *spiffy* means?"
Bertie had heard that word before.

He wiggled his tooth
and tried to remember where.
No one in the class raised a hand.
"Find out over the weekend,"
Mrs. Hughes said.
"Tell me on Monday."

BERTIE REMEMBERS

Bertie thought all the way home.
He wiggled his loose tooth back and forth
and back and forth while he thought.
At last he remembered.

It was before his grandparents
moved to Florida.
He was staying at their house.
Everyone was getting dressed up
to go out to dinner.
Bertie and his gramps looked just alike.
They both wore gray pants.
They both wore white shirts.
They both wore blue jackets.

And they both wore red polka-dot bow ties.
"Don't you two look spiffy!"
Gram said when she saw them.

Now Bertie knew what he would wear
for his picture on Monday.
When Mrs. Hughes saw him
in his red polka-dot bow tie,
she would think he looked spiffy, too.

Bertie smiled a wide smile as he thought about it.

Just then Howard called,

"Hey, Bertie!"

Bertie turned, still smiling.

WOMP!

A kickball hit him right in the face.

"Did it work this time?" Howard asked.

Bertie tasted blood in his mouth.

He felt something like a little stone
on his tongue.
He spit it out into his hand.
"Hooray!" shouted Howard.
"At last!" said Bertie.
He smiled and slipped the tooth
into his pocket.
Then Bertie stuck the tip of his tongue
through the square hole
the missing teeth made.
"Cool!" said Howard.
"Do that for your picture on Monday!"
Bertie laughed and said good-bye.
Then he ran all the way home
so he could see his new square hole
in the mirror.

SHINER

TIN MONEY

When Bertie woke up on Saturday morning,
he looked under his pillow.
There was a shiny silver dollar
and a small folded note.
Bertie stuck his tongue
through his new square hole while he read.

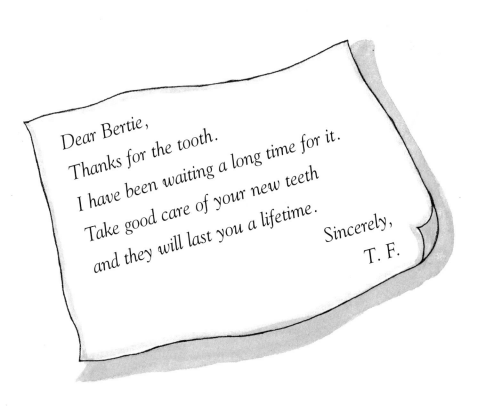

Dear Bertie,
Thanks for the tooth.
I have been waiting a long time for it.
Take good care of your new teeth
and they will last you a lifetime.

Sincerely,
T. F.

Bertie reached under his bed.

He pulled out a round red tin.

Keemun Black Tea was printed on the side.

The tin rattled when Bertie moved it.

He pulled off the top.

There were three silver dollars inside—
one for each tooth Bertie had lost.
There were three notes inside, too.
The notes were all signed T. F.
Bertie put the new note
and silver dollar in the tin.
He slid the tin back under his bed.
He wondered how many silver dollars
he would have when all his teeth fell out.
Maybe he would have enough to buy
a new bike!

He smiled, got dressed,
and went downstairs for breakfast.

STRAW TRICKS

"Do we have any straws?"
Bertie asked his mother.
"Straws?" his mother said.
"Check in the towel drawer."
Bertie found a box of plastic straws
left over from his last birthday party.
He put one in his glass of milk.
He took the glass over
to the mirror by the back door.
He smiled widely and slipped the straw
through the square hole.
He sipped some milk and slipped
the straw out.
He smiled again and slipped the straw in.

Eloise came over and watched him.

"I want a straw, too," she said.

"They're in the towel drawer,"
Bertie told her.

"But you won't be able to do this trick."

Eloise got a straw.

She grinned hard at the mirror.

She pushed the straw
against her front teeth.

She tried to squeeze it
through her side teeth.

She opened her teeth a little bit
and slid it in.
When she pulled the straw out,
it was squished flat.

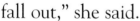

"Face it, Eloise," Bertie said.
"You need a square hole to do this trick.
And you are not going to let
your teeth fall out.
Remember?"
"I remember," said Eloise.
She looked at her teeth in the mirror.
"But maybe I will let just two teeth
fall out," she said.

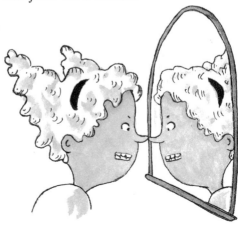

Just then the phone rang.

It was Howard.

"We're going to the park to play kickball.

Want to come?"

Bertie called to his mom to ask

if he could go.

"All right," she called back.

"Sure," Bertie told Howard.

"I'll meet you there soon."

When Bertie got off the phone,

Eloise said,

"Can I come, Bertie?

I like to play kickball.

I can kick hard.

I can run fast.

Please, please, please, can I come?"

Bertie wanted to say no.
But his mother said,
"It would be really nice
if you let Eloise play with you."
Bertie let out a big sigh.
"Okay, Eloise. You can come."

WHO'S ON FIRST?

After Bertie showed his friends
his square hole,
they all formed teams.
Bertie's team had four kids:
Bertie, Isobel, Patrick, and Molly.
Howard's team had four kids, too:
Howard, Daniel, Amanda, and Eloise.

Howard was the best player.
He kicked the ball harder than anyone.
He ran faster than anyone, too.
He made up for Eloise.

Eloise didn't kick very hard.
Sometimes she even missed the ball
when she was supposed to kick it.
She didn't run very fast, either.
But she didn't give up.

Howard and Eloise's team
was winning 10 to 8.
It was Eloise's turn to kick.
Bertie guarded first base.
Easy out, he thought.
Patrick rolled the ball to Eloise.
Eloise ran to meet it.
She kicked it hard.
It rolled between first base
and the pitcher's spot.

Patrick thought Bertie would get it.

Bertie thought Patrick would get it.

At last Bertie ran for the ball.

He scooped it up and ran hard

for first base.

Eloise was running hard, too.

Would Eloise get to first base

before Bertie?

Then she would be safe.

Would Bertie get there first

and tag the base?

Then Eloise would be out.

Two Out

Eloise didn't get to the base first.

But Bertie didn't get there first, either.

They got there at the same time.

CRASH!

Their heads banged together.

"Ouch!" cried Bertie.

He covered his right eye with both hands.

"Ow! Ow! Ow!" cried Eloise.

She held both hands over her mouth.

All the other kids ran over to help.

They saw blood on Eloise's hands.

"Uh-oh," said Howard.

Eloise pulled her hands away
from her mouth.

Tears spilled down her cheeks.
She spit something out.
It was a tooth.
She spit again.
It was another tooth.
"Bertie! My teeth!" Eloise cried.
She opened her hand
to show Bertie the two teeth.
She opened her mouth
to show Bertie the new space.

"Two out at once!" said Bertie.
"Way to go, Eloise!" said Howard.
Eloise wiped away her tears.
She held the two teeth
tightly in her hand.
They all walked home.

ICE HELPS

"Oh, my goodness!
What happened?" their mother cried.
"I lost two teeth," said Eloise.
She pulled down her bottom lip
to show her mother.
"It was an accident," said Bertie.
"We bumped heads really hard.
We were both trying to get to first base."

"My lip feels funny," said Eloise.
Her mom gave her some ice
wrapped in a towel.
"The ice will help," she told Eloise.
"The whole side of my face feels funny,"
said Bertie.

"Ice will help that, too," she said.

"But I think you may have a shiner, Bertie."

"What's a shiner?" Bertie asked.

"A black eye," his mother told him.

"Cool!" said Bertie.

He had never had a black eye before.

THE MORNING AFTER

Bertie looked in the mirror
when he woke up.
The skin around his eye was black,
puffy, and shiny.
So that's why they call it a shiner,
he thought.
He pressed it gently.
It hurt, but not too much.
He went downstairs for breakfast.

Eloise ran into the kitchen.
"Look!" she cried.
"I got two silver dollars
from the Tooth Fairy.

Read the note to me, Bertie."

Bertie unfolded the note, and read:

Dear Eloise,
What a surprise!
Two teeth out in one day!
Take your time losing the rest.
I'm not in a hurry to get them.
Sincerely,
T. F.

Bertie looked at his little sister.

"I'm sorry I knocked out your teeth, Eloise.",

Eloise gave him a gap-toothed smile.

"That's okay, Bertie.

It was an accident," she said.

"I'm sorry I gave you a shiner."

"That was an accident, too,"

Bertie told her.

"The same accident," he said, and laughed.

Bertie thought about the new bike

he wanted to buy with his tooth money.

Then he pulled a silver dollar

and a note from his pocket.

"I found this in my room," he told Eloise.
"I think it's for you."
Eloise's eyes grew big
when she looked at the silver dollar.
"Read it to me, Bertie," she asked.

Bertie read:

Dear Eloise,
I'm glad you changed your mind
about losing your teeth.
Try the trick with the straw again.
I think it might work.

Sincerely,
T. F.'s Helper

Eloise and Bertie went to the mirror.
They had glasses of milk and straws.

Bertie smiled and slid the straw
into his mouth.
Eloise smiled,
squeezed her straw a little,
and slid it into her mouth, too.
It was a close fit, but it worked—
just like T. F.'s Helper said it would.

A TERRIBLY
INTERESTING HAIRCUT

ELOISE MAKES A PLAN

It was Sunday.
Bertie was reading the comics.
Eloise was standing at the mirror.
She was combing her hair
with a new red comb.

"Guess what, Bertie?" Eloise said.
"What?" asked Bertie.
"I know what I want to be
when I grow up," she said.
"I know what you want to be
when you grow up, too.
An airplane pilot,
like Donna Jensen's dad," Bertie said.
"That was before." said Eloise.

"Now I want to be a hairstylist.
I will have my own shop,
just like Cindy Miller's mother.
I will cut, comb, and curl
to help people look their best.
When people look their best,
they are happier.
A good hairstylist
can make the world a happier place."

"Let me guess," said Bertie.
"Did Mrs. Miller visit your class on Friday?"
"Yes," said Eloise.

"Fridays are
Bring-Your-Parent-to-School Day.
And she gave all of us
red combs and red lollipops."
"And now you want to be a hairstylist
when you grow up?" Bertie asked.
"Yup," said Eloise.

"Well, Eloise, I'm sorry I won't be flying
in your plane with you someday."
"Don't be sorry, Bertie.
Just let me cut your hair," she said.
"Okay, Eloise.
Someday you can cut my hair.
But now I'm reading the comics.
So could you please stop talking to me?"

BERTIE GIVES IN

"Could I at least comb your hair?"
Eloise asked.
"Oh, Eloise . . .," Bertie said.
"I'm reading the comics now.
I don't want to have my hair combed."
Eloise was quiet for a minute.
Then she said,
"Well, I didn't want
to have my teeth knocked out.
But you did it anyway."

Bertie rolled his eyes.
"Oh, all right," he said.
"Comb my hair."

Eloise pulled the comb
through Bertie's hair.
"Ouch!" said Bertie.
"That's too hard, Eloise."

Eloise tried again.
"Ow!" Bertie cried.
"It hurts."
"Okay, now I know
what I was doing wrong," Eloise said.
"It won't hurt anymore.
I promise."

She began to comb Bertie's hair again.

"Eloise, stop!

It feels like you're pulling the hair

right out of my head."

"I only pulled out a little," Eloise told him.

"And it was an accident."

Bertie grabbed the comb from her hand.

"No more accidents," Bertie told her.

"No more pulling.

No more combing!"

He slammed the comb

down onto the table.

"You are a terrible customer, Bertie,"

Eloise told him.

A Book and a Nap

Bertie went to his room.

He liked to lie on his bed and read.

He had gotten a book from

the library on Friday.

He was looking forward to reading it.

He hoped it would be funny.

Before he began to read,

he looked at himself in the mirror.

He smiled and admired his square hole.

He looked at his black eye.

It was a little bit yellow around the edges.

He touched it gently.

It was still tender.

Bertie read for a long time.

Sometimes the book was funny.

Sometimes it was sad.

He wanted to know how it ended.

But he didn't want it to be over.

When he was finished, he closed his eyes.

Before he knew it, he had fallen asleep.

Bertie dreamed he was in an airplane.

Eloise was the pilot.

He could feel the wind blowing

through his hair.

He could hear Eloise saying,

"A little over here.

A little over there."

Bertie felt a spider crawl across his face.

When he tried to brush it away,

he woke up.

There was no airplane.

There was no wind in his hair.

There was no spider on his face.

But there was Eloise, and she was holding

safety scissors and her new red comb.

Bertie was wide awake now.

He sat up in his bed and gasped.

ELOISE'S FIRST HAIRCUT

There was hair all over his pillow.

There was hair all over his bed.

It was his hair.

"Eloise!

What are you doing?" Bertie cried.

"I'm cutting your hair.

You said I could cut your hair,"

she told him.

"I said you could cut my hair *someday*.

Someday when you know how to cut hair!"

Bertie climbed out of bed

and went to his mirror.

There were big chunks of hair

missing from his head.

"Oh, no, Eloise," Bertie moaned.

"This looks terrible!"

Eloise's eyes filled with tears.

"I can fix it," she said.

"I don't want you to look terrible."

"No!" Bertie shouted.

"You've done too much already."

He took the scissors from her hands.

Two fat tears slid down Eloise's cheeks.

"I don't think you look terrible, Bertie.

I think you look . . ."

Eloise stared at her brother for a minute.

"Like Henry!" she cried.

"Henry?" Bertie asked.

He looked at himself in the mirror again.

A Sick Dog Haircut

Henry had been Bertie's grandparent's dog.
Before he died,
Henry got sick and his fur
fell out in clumps.
Eloise was right.
Bertie looked very much
like Henry right now.

"Henry was a good dog,
wasn't he, Bertie?" Eloise asked.
Bertie smiled as he remembered.
"The best," Bertie told her.
Eloise sniffed back more tears.
"Do you really think your haircut

is terrible, Bertie?" she asked.

Bertie took a deep breath and sighed.

"Did I say this was a terrible haircut?"
Bertie asked.

"I meant . . . terribly interesting."

Eloise smiled a tiny, sad smile.

"This is a terribly
interesting haircut, Eloise."

"So, you like it?" Eloise asked.

Hope gleamed in her eyes.

Bertie took another deep breath.

"Don't push it, Eloise," he said.

Bertie went downstairs.

He wanted to eat something
to take his mind off his hair.

He got out a bowl of cereal.

He poured lots of cold milk on it.

He was half done when his mother came in.

"Oh, good heavens, Bertie!

What did you do to your hair?"

"I didn't do anything to my hair," he said.

"Eloise did something to my hair.

She wants to be a hairstylist

when she grows up.

"First I told her it was terrible.

But when she started to cry,

I said something else.

I told her it was terribly interesting.

She thinks she did a good job.

I'm just glad she doesn't want to be

a heart surgeon.

I would probably be bleeding
to death right now."

His mother hid a smile behind her hand.
"The barbershop isn't open on Sunday,
Bertie," his mother told him.
"But I'll take you there
right after school on Monday."

She started to leave the kitchen.
Then she turned back.
"Bertie, I think Eloise is very lucky
to have you for a big brother."
Bertie rolled his eyes
and poured another bowl of cereal.

PICTURE DAY

SPIFFY

On Monday morning Bertie woke up
bright and early.
He remembered that it was Picture Day.
He remembered that Mrs. Hughes
told them to look spiffy.
He remembered exactly what
he would wear.

He got out of bed,
went over to his mirror, and smiled.
He liked the square hole
where his front teeth were missing.
He looked at his shiner.
It wasn't just black.
It was blue, purple, and yellow, too.

He looked at his terrible, sick-dog haircut.
He thought about Eloise
and rolled his eyes.
He thought about Henry
and smiled.
Henry was a good dog.
Bertie missed him.

Then Bertie got dressed.
He put on his gray pants.
He put on his white shirt.
He put on his blue jacket.
He put on his red polka-dot bow tie.
He thought about his grandparents
in Florida.
Bertie missed them, too.

He took one last look in the mirror.
"Spiffy," he said to himself with a grin.
He went downstairs for breakfast.

His mom raised her eyebrows
when she saw Bertie.
"Why so dressed up today, sweetie?"
she asked.
"Today is Picture Day," Bertie told her.
He pulled the crumpled paper
from his backpack.

"Picture Day?" said his mother.
"And you have a black eye!
And a haircut that's so . . ."
She looked at Eloise.

"Terribly interesting," Bertie said.

"Yes," said his mother.

"Terribly interesting."

She planted a kiss right in the middle
of Bertie's terribly interesting haircut.

"I'm sure you'll take
a great picture, Bertie," she said.

Very Spiffy Indeed

Bertie and his classmates took their seats.

Molly raised her hand.

"Mrs. Hughes?" she called.

"I found out what *spiffy* means.

It means all dressed up and looking good!"

Mrs. Hughes smiled at her class.

She looked at each child and nodded.

When she looked at Bertie,

her eyes opened wide.

"Bertie!

Did you get hurt this weekend?"

she asked.

"Yes," said Bertie.

"I got a shiner in a kickball game."

"Tell her what happened to your hair,"
said Howard.

Bertie felt the top of his head.

"My little sister, Eloise, did it," he said.

"She wants to be a hairstylist
and make the world a happier place.
She's not very good yet."

Mrs. Hughes smiled.

"Well, I think you all look wonderful.
Very spiffy indeed!"

One day a few weeks later,
Bertie's pictures came back.
His shiner was all healed now.
His terribly interesting haircut
had been trimmed by a barber.
His bottom teeth were starting
to fill in his square hole.
He looked at his picture.
He remembered the day it was taken.
It seemed like a long time ago.

That night he sent a picture and a letter
to his grandparents.

He wrote:

Dear Gram and Gramps,
Here I am with my square hole,
my first shiner,
and Eloise's first haircut.
Pretty spiffy, don't you think?

Love,
Bertie

The End